TUESDAY

Mr. Bumba's
TUESDAY CLUB

By Pearl Augusta Harwood

Pictures by Joseph Folger

Published by Lerner Publications Company · Minneapolis, Minnesota

The type used
in this book is
MR. BUMBA TEXT
set in 16 point.

Standard Book Number: 8225-0110-4
Library of Congress Catalog Card Number: 65-27998

Third Printing 1970

On Tuesday, after school, Bill and Lee and Jane were visiting Mr. Bumba.

Mr. Bumba was sitting at his easel in the sunroom. He was painting a picture of high mountains, so they sat still and watched him.

"There," said Mr. Bumba. "I think that is all I shall do today. Let's have some buns."

They ate cinnamon buns with raisins on top.

Jane looked at a picture of some houses. It was on the wall of Mr. Bumba's sunroom.

"I'd like to make a picture of Peppy's and Brownie's henhouse," said Jane. "But I don't know how to make the roof look right. Will you show me how?"

Mr. Bumba put a paper on his other easel and let Jane try the paints. Then he helped her with the roof of her house.

Bill and Lee were watching.

"I wish I could do that, too," said Bill. "My houses always look crooked."

"And mine always look flat," said Lee.

"Well, well," said Mr. Bumba. "I guess we need some more easels."

They looked around the room.

"There is a long piece of soft wallboard," said Jane.

"Yes, I was cutting that in pieces, to hang pictures on," said Mr. Bumba. "That piece is eight feet long."

He scratched his head. "If we could put it up on a chair—" he said.

"We could put it on <u>two</u> chairs," said Lee.

They put the piece of wallboard across two chairs. It made a good easel. Three people could work there.

Mr. Bumba put thumbtacks in some large papers for Bill and Lee. Then Jane moved her paper over to the new easel.

They all tried drawing the roofs of houses, and Mr. Bumba helped them.

"Now you are all doing very well," said Mr. Bumba.

"I wish we could do this one day every week," said Bill.

"Painting lessons are fun," said Jane.

"Could we do errands for you, to pay for our painting lessons?" asked Lee.

"Well, now, maybe we could have a Tuesday afternoon painting club," said Mr. Bumba with a wide smile. "And I do need a lot of errands done, every once in a while."

"Could we come and paint next Tuesday?" asked Jane.

"Certainly," said Mr. Bumba.

But even before next Tuesday came, Jane
and Bill and Lee went visiting Mr. Bumba
again. On Friday, they rode their bicycles
over to the pasture of Peppy the burro. They
all had rides on Peppy's back. They helped
Mr. Bumba feed the burro. They helped clean
his house. They also petted Brownie the hen.

"My friend Ann wishes she could be in the Tuesday afternoon painting club," said Jane. "Ann showed me how to ride her bicycle a while ago."

"My friend Jack wishes he could be in it, too," said Bill.

"My friend Allen said so, too," said Lee.

Mr. Bumba scratched his head. "I suppose a club is more fun if more people are in it," he said.

"We'd need another piece of wallboard for another big easel," said Bill.

"I have another piece in my garage," said Mr. Bumba.

They went back to Mr. Bumba's garage and looked inside.

"You have two old chairs here, to put the wallboard on," said Lee.

"Could we bring our snacks to eat, after the painting lesson is over?" asked Jane.

"I suppose people do like to eat at club meetings," said Mr. Bumba. "I could make some Bumba tea."

"Bumba tea!" said Lee and Bill and Jane. "What's that?"

Mr. Bumba smiled a wide smile.

"Bumba tea is different every time I make it," he said.

"My mother doesn't let me drink regular tea," said Jane.

"Oh, this isn't regular tea," said Mr. Bumba.

"But what is it?" asked Lee.

"Is it just sugar and water?" asked Bill. "I don't like that very much."

"Oh, no," said Mr. Bumba. "But it does have hot water."

They all laughed. "Who ever heard of tea without hot water!" said Jane.

"And brown sugar," said Mr. Bumba. "Always brown sugar."

"What else does it have?" asked Lee.

"Well," said Mr. Bumba, "sometimes it has orange juice.

"Sometimes it has lemon juice.

"Sometimes it has lime juice.

"Sometimes it has pineapple juice.

"Sometimes it has grape juice.

"Or any two of those things, or any three, or any four, or even <u>all</u> <u>five.</u>"

"Goodness, how many different ways can you make it?" asked Jane.

"You'd be surprised," said Mr. Bumba. "There are more different ways than I can even count."

Bill and Lee and Jane all tried to count the different ways, but it was too hard. They gave up.

"I think it would be nice to have a different kind of Bumba tea every single time the club meets," said Jane.

On Monday, Jane came over to Mr. Bumba's house.

"My mother will buy all the paints we need to use in our painting club," she told Mr. Bumba.

Pretty soon Bill came over.

"My mother will buy all the paintbrushes we need to use in the painting club," he said.

Soon afterwards, Lee came.

"My father works at the newspaper office," said Lee. "He can get us all the blank paper we want to use for painting."

"My goodness!" said Mr. Bumba. "I shall not have to buy anything at all!"

"You are doing too much for us already," said Jane. "That's what my mother said."

On Tuesday afternoon, Mr. Bumba was all ready for the painting club.

There was room for six people to paint at the two long easels in the sunroom.

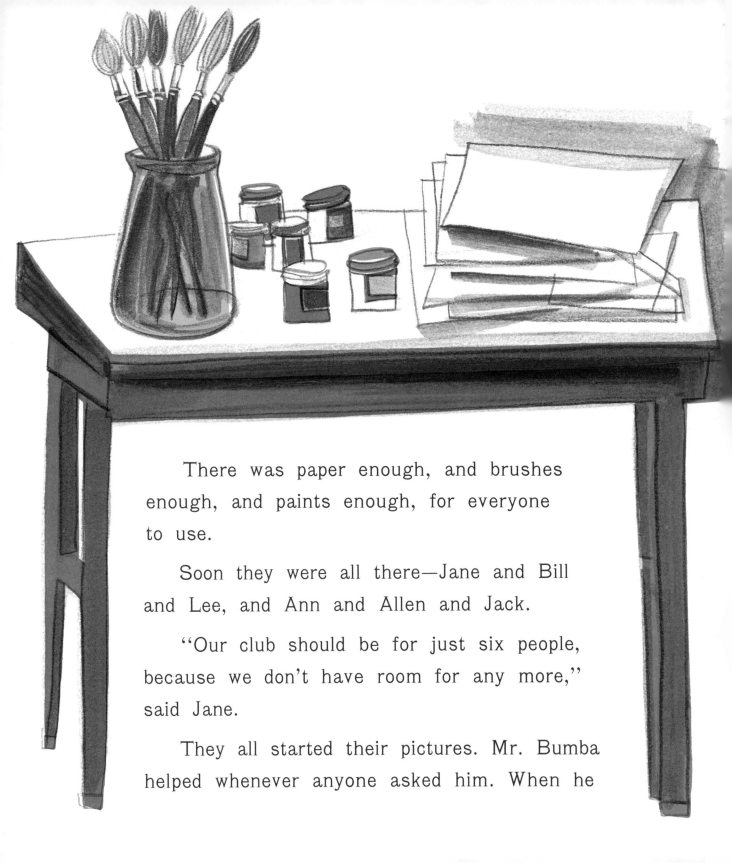

There was paper enough, and brushes enough, and paints enough, for everyone to use.

Soon they were all there—Jane and Bill and Lee, and Ann and Allen and Jack.

"Our club should be for just six people, because we don't have room for any more," said Jane.

They all started their pictures. Mr. Bumba helped whenever anyone asked him. When he

was not helping someone, he worked on his
own picture at his own easel.

Jane painted another house, with a very
good roof on it.

Ann painted some children playing at the
seashore.

Jack painted a picture of his dog.

Allen painted a baseball game.

Bill painted a street in the city at night.

Lee was painting something, but he did not ask Mr. Bumba to help. No one saw his picture. They were all busy with their own painting.

After a while, Mr. Bumba walked over to see what Lee was doing. Mr. Bumba began to laugh and laugh. He laughed so hard that he had to wipe his eyes.

Everyone else came to look at Lee's painting. They all laughed and laughed.

"It looks just like Mr. Bumba!" said Jane.

"It does look like me," said Mr. Bumba.

"That is just how you looked when you were learning to ride a bicycle!" said Bill.

"Lee can draw people," said Mr. Bumba. "He can make a picture look like the real person. Maybe he will be a cartoonist some day!"

"Let's have Lee for the president of our painting club," said Jane. "Every club has a president."

The others thought that was a fine idea.

"Then if I'm president," said Lee, "I
move we stop painting and eat our snacks.
After we clean up, of course."

They all agreed. Each one cleaned up the
mess he had made. They washed the paintbrushes.

Then they sat down on Mr. Bumba's three chairs and three stools, with their snacks on the table. The snacks were buns from Mrs. Abby's bakery. They had each brought a cup and a spoon. Mr. Bumba had the fourth chair.

"What kind of Bumba tea is it today?" asked Jane.

"Guess," said Mr. Bumba.

They all guessed, but no one got it quite right.

"I'll have to tell you," said Mr. Bumba, smiling a very wide smile.

"Wait—one more guess," said Jane. "I guess that you put <u>everything</u> in this time —lemon, orange, lime, pineapple, and grape juices all together!"

"That is exactly the right guess," said Mr. Bumba. He went to the stove and began to pour tea out of his big kettle.

"I know three boys who wish they could come to this club," said Bill.

"Doris and Mary Smith wish they could come," said Jane.

"And Eva and Bunny and Kate," said Ann.

"And David and Martin and Dick," said Lee.

"Oh, my goodness!" said Mr. Bumba. "All those boys and girls want to have painting lessons?"

"Of course we told them they couldn't," said Bill.

"There isn't room for anyone else," said Jane.

"Wait a minute," said Mr. Bumba. "I feel an idea coming."

"If we could ever paint outdoors—" said Lee.

"When summer vacation comes—" said Bill.

"You are getting my idea!" said Mr. Bumba.

"Each person could pay for his own paper and paints and brushes," said Lee.

"But where would we get enough easels?" asked Jane.

"That's the rest of my idea," said Mr. Bumba. "Look out in my backyard."

They all got up and went to look out the window.

"I don't see anything but the fence, all around the yard," said Jane.

"That's it, the fence!" cried Lee.

Mr. Bumba smiled. "We can put papers
up on the fence with thumbtacks," he said.
"It won't hurt the fence. It won't hurt the
pictures I have painted there. It won't hurt my
garden, for that is in the middle of the yard."

"We could have twenty people in the summer vacation painting club!" said Lee.

"And summer vacation is coming in two more months!" said Bill.

Jane was thinking. "Pretty soon the days will be too hot to have Bumba tea," she said.

"We could put ice in it, and make Bumba punch," said Lee.

"Hooray!" said Bill. "We'll tell all those people tomorrow."

"It's a little Tuesday club now, but it will be a big Tuesday club then," said Jane.

"The Bumba summer painting club," said Lee.

They all clapped their hands.

Then they had some more Bumba tea.